Hours of Darkness

Flairs and Glairs

Publication House

"Hours of Darkness"

ISBN No: " 9789391302160"
1st Edition
Language – English and Hindi

Flairs and Glairs
Publication House
Regd. Under MSME Act.

Disclaimer

This is a work of fiction and solely represent the thoughts of the corresponding authors of the articles. Our editors have tried their best to edit the content of all the authors and check the plagiarism.

All the write-ups in this book are unique and are only published in this book.

In case any plagiarism or error is found, only the author is responsible alone, and not the publisher or the Compilers.

Cover Designing and Book Formatting
Shubham Shah and Ishani Agarwal

Co-Authors

1. Arghya Sengupta
2. Arun Anukrati
3. Arushi Dhar
4. Bandhuli Chatterjee
5. Divyanshu Rai
6. Iti Verma
7. Manya Arora
8. Nishant
9. Priyanka K. Tiwari
10. Renukuntla Murali
11. Ritwika Ghosh
12. Sanjay Naik
13. Siddharth Agarwal
14. Suriyanshi Mishra
15. T. Priyadharshini
16. Taniya Khemchandani
17. Trupti Rajesh Hangirgekar
18. Venessa Albuquerque
19. Yashikakaramchandani
20. Zainab Shaki

Shubham Shah

(Founder - Flairs and Glairs)

Shubham Shah, an entrepreneur at "Flairs & Glairs" a brand with dynamics in events organizing and cultural educational pan INDIA, is a 26yrs old guy who recently has entered the digital platform of imprinting emotions. He has initiated with his own open mic platform to hel p budding poets and aspiring writers under his brand named as "Teekhe Zasbaaat"

He is a commerce graduate from the Bhagalpur City of Bihar.

He states Writing has impersonated him since childhood and he has now been writing for over a decade!

Cooking, on the other hand, is his passion! He also mentions, trying out new things just tickles him!

When asked sir, Why SPICY EMOTIONS?

He smiled and added, "agar jasbaat teekhe na ho toh wo jasbaat kahan" Spices are all that blends! So do his words!

As a chef, he presents to you his dish! Hot and freshly served! Taste it! Feel it! Enjoy it! You can also find his writing in the Book "Teekhe Zasbaaat" and 50+ Co -authored anthologies. With his passion to explore opportunities across Platforms, he is working with keen dev   otion and We wish him all the very best for his future ventures.

He is Featured in the International Magazine DeMode for his upcoming solo novel.

He is Approved by Ne8x for its Lit Fest, and is a Golden Star Awards 2020 Winner.

He is a India Book of Records Holder for his Anthology Satrang, and has the Grandmaster title by Asia Book of Records, for the same.

He has also been featured in Prabhat Khabar, Dainik Jagran, and a lot of other Newspapers in Bihar for his achievements.

He has been a proud co-author to

India Book Of Records (Title- Black)

World Book Of Records (Title -15 Wonders of Poetries)

India Book Of Records (Title - Aaina)

Vajra World Records Holder (Title - Gustakhi Maaf Hai)

High Range of Records Holder (Title - Gustakhi Maaf Hai)

Indian Book of Records

(Title - Road from Worst to Best)

Share your reviews on his

INSTAGRAM

@spicy_emotions
@shubham4shah

Or via email on

shubham2shah@gmail.com

To stay tuned to his work and opportunities follow his business Handles

INSTAGRAM   FACEBOOK   YOUTUBE

@flairsandglairs
@teekhezasbaaat

WEBSITE:

https://flairsandglairs.in/
https://flairsandglairs.com/

Ishani Agarwal

(Co-Founder- Flairs and Glairs)

Ishani Agarwal hails from the City of Joy, Kolkata.
She is the co -founder of her Community "Teekhe Zasbaaat" and Flairs and Glairs Publication.
Been a Compiler for 45+ Anthologies, she is in the process for more. Co -authored in 150+ Anthologies. She is a India Book of Records Holder, a Vajra World Records Holder, a High Range of Records Holder,   an OMG Book of Records Holder, a Bravo Record holder, a Forever Star Book of World Records and an Indian Book of Records Holder.
Approved by Ne8x for its Lit Fest 2020, and Literary Icon 2020. Also a Golden Star Awards Winner 2020.
She has also been award ed with India Star Republic Award 2021, a part of She Awards by Awards Arc and Winner of Nari Samman 2021 by Literoma.

She is also selected as Best Achiever of the Year by AwardsArc and Most Challenging Compiler Award by Spectrum Awards.
She got her first solo Published,a solo Compilation consisting of first 750 contents of hers, titled "Hand That Burnt While Healing".

She has been featured by the National Magazine "Taree Zameen Par" with the title 'unstoppable'.
Also featured in the International Magazine DeMode for her upcoming solo novel, she is proud to write on social issues, and is happy with the love she is receiving.
Connect with her on Instagram: @Ishani_agarwal_quotes / @compilations_so_far

Mita Das
(Compiler)

Mita Das is a creative writer who loves to write about everything she loves. A teacher by profession and a passionate writer. Apart from writing,she loves dancing and painting. She co -authored in several anthologies and few of them are record holders. A Potterhead and a nerd. You can follow her on instagram, her instagram id is @almost.cr8ive.

Goddess Kali

Sulekha devi was very happy that day, she was getting ready to visit a girl's family for marriage, her son also accompanied her. Sulekha devi decided that if she found the girl beautiful, she will fix the marriage. She came from the house, dressed beautifully. Before leaving, she went to the Goddess Kali temple, that was situated beside her house, to seek blessings. After doing a puja she came out of the temple and was walking by the road, when a small girl in shabby dress appeared in front of her, she begged in front of her, but she literally shooed her away saying, " Go away from here you ugly girl." She gave alms to poor generally, but the girl was of dark complexion, and she hated anyone, whose complexion was dark.

When she went to the girl's house, she didn't stay there for a minute and came out with her son, the reason was, the complexion of the girl was also dark. Sulekha devi was very disturbed, she was unable to find a girl for her son. She went to the temple once again, but she was shocked when she entered inside. She couldn't see the idol of the goddess Kali, she asked the purohit "What happened? Where is the idol of the goddess." The purohit found her behaviour strange, he said " It is here only" even her son agreed with the purohit, but she was unable to see. Her dark mind, dark ment   ality completely blinded her vision.O ne can't see Goddess Kali with dark mind, dark heart and dark mentality?

The Night Sky

There was a power cut all of a sudden when she was doing a very important work. She had to finish her work before the deadline, but the sudden power cut made it impossible. To add her irritation, all her documents were saved in the desktop and she needed those documents to complete her work. The dark room frustrated her, so she came out from the room and stood in the balcony, she found that the whole locality was immersed in darkness, but her irritation vanished when she looked at the sky.

The full moon looked like a pearl in   the dark sky and the twinkling stars increased it's beauty. The sky looked like a beautiful black gown, decorated with diamonds and pearls. She remembered that she used to adore the night sky in the same manner when she was a child, but adulthood snatched away those little pleasures from her. She decided to write something after a long time, she took out her phone, opened the notepad and wrote a poem after a long time. She wrote a poem.

After a long time her heart was filled with the light of the moon and the beauty of the stars. She felt that a great burden was released from her heart after a long time.
Only a dark sky can gift you the stars and the Moon. Sometimes darkness is required to understand the beauty of light.

"Darkness feels like home when   the restless heart becomes free from all the chaos and the imprisoned thoughts flow freely in the calmness of the dark."

Khushi Agrawal
(Compiler)

KHUSHI AGRAWAL is 20 -year-old girl living in Fort - Songadh, Gujarat. She is B.tech ICT student.

She is co-author in 20+ anthology, including record holding anthology.

She is compiler of 5+ anthology.

She likes reading fiction novels and autobiography. Her ambition is to crack UPSC CSE exams.

You can join her on khushi2712.ka@gmail.com.

IG @a.khushi2704

(1)

The late-night hours,
Under the dark sky,
Looking at the starts,
Holding Your hand tight,
You kissing my forehead,
Each day
These are best HOURS OF DARKNESS,
Of my day.

-Hours of Darkness

(2)

You came in my life
Like a blissful morning,
After the longest dark night,
Of my life.

-It's only you

Arghya Sengupta

Arghya Sengupta from Nashik, Maharashtra, aged 18 is a budding writer. He has started writing just few months back and now writing is one of his hobbies.

The Broken Words

No one sees pain, no one sees grief, no one sees what's fair, but everyone sees your mistakes. And that's the darkest fact.
"You are a disappointment"
They said under their breath.
As those who said they cared about her just got up and left. So her wrists turned into canvases and brushes turned into blades. And her paintings turned to waterfalls where often blood would shed. And the brightness in her eyes started to dim and slowly left. And soon the sunshine in her eyes turned into rain and wept.
"I am okay."
And everyone believed her and went out of her way. But soon her voice got quieter and she seemed much less sure. And she dropped her fake smile and said,
"I don't care anymore."

Today, it's been hard, pretending I'm okay. Wanting to cry so hard so I just have to breathe and carry on. Smile. It's gonna be okay they say, it gets better they say, you got this they say. But what if it's not okay? And what if I haven't got this? What do I do then huh? All I can see is Darkness...

You might think I am strong but I am hiding my emotions from everyone including you, you think I am honest with you about everything but I know no one is strong enough for me and my problems.

Arun Anukrati

अरुण अनुकृति (अनुकृति श्रीवास्तव) एक मेकैनिकल इंजीनियर हैं जो कई वर्षों से अध्यापन के क्षेत्र में कार्यरत हैं| बचपन में अपने पिता, अरुण श्रीवास्तव को अख़बारों और पत्रिकाओं के लिए कई लेख लिखते देख इनकी लेखन में रुचि जागृत हुई और अपने कार्यक्षेत्र में कई बार छात्रों को प्रोत्साहित करते समय इन्हें शब्दों की शक्ति का एहसास हुआ| इनका लक्ष्य अब अपने लेखन से लोगों को मानसिक शांति देना ओर उनकी हिम्मत बढ़ाना है| वे इससे पहले भी बारह अलग-अलग संकलनों का हिस्सा रह चुकी हैं|

"कर्मयोगी"

अपने हाथों की ओट में मेहनत का दीप जलाया था,
कर दूंगी दूर अंधेरा मैं, कुछ यूँ विश्वास जगाया था|

भाग्य ने परखा बहुत, अब कर्म परखने आया था;
हर मुश्किल से लड़ने का ही जज़्बा मुझमें पाया था|

अंधियारे ने तंज कसा कि कैसे राह बनाओगी,
मेरे जीते-जी सोचो, क्या तुम आगे बढ़ पाओगी?

तब हंसी गूंजी थी उसकी, अब मेरे नाम का शोर है;
सफलता से जुड़ी कर्मों की कुछ ऐसी ही डोर है!

जितना इसे तानोगे तुम, ये पक्की भी उतनी होगी,
पग-पग में अपने डर पर जीत हासिल करनी होगी|

विनयशील जो कर्मरत हो, बाधा उसका क्या हरे?
कर्मों का तेज जो साथ लिये, अंधेरों में वो क्यों घिरे?

न हो उत्साह सफलता का न हार में उत्तेजित मन है,
उसकी हर पूंजी सदैव ही परोपकार को अर्पण है|

एक कर्मयोगी के लिए सदा ही सब कुछ एक समान है,
क्या अंधेरा, क्या प्रकाश, जब चित्त में 'वो' विद्यमान है|

"अंधकार से सफलता"

क्यों रात की तनहाई में याद का दीपक जलता है?
किसीका साथ न होना क्यों इस दिल को खलता है?

अकेले में आंखों से आंसू बन क्यों दर्द निकलता है?
क्यों अतीत की स्मृतियों में वर्तमान यूँ जलता है?

समय का पहिया एक गति से अनवरत ही चलता है
सूरज भी सबकी राहें रोशन कर प्रतिदिन ढलता है|

नया भाव, आंखों में सपना नव हर दिन ही पलता है
हम रोशनी की ओर बढें तो अंधेरा पीछे चलता है|

प्रकाश की पूजा सब करते हैं अंधकार में निर्बलता है,
चकाचौंध में खो जाना भी तो कर्म की विफलता है|

कदमों की गति बढ़ जाती है जब अंधेरा निकलता है
क्यों नकारें कि बेहतरी सिर्फ अंधेरे की कुशलता है?

चलते-चलते ठोकर खाकर फिर इंसान संभलता है,
हर दिन थोड़ा बेहतर बनना ही वास्तविक सफलता है|

Arushi Dhar

An amateur writer from Ahmedabad India, Arushi Dhar began to write poems believing that the universe holds so many stories to tell. She wrote them for shaping her thoughts and channelizing them as her superpower. That's how she started her Instagram page @ _thepoetspoet.

Ye Jo Gehri Kaali Raatein Hai

Kabhi sapno se jo shuru hua karti thi
Wo raatein
Aaj kal kisi ko khone ke darr mein jeeti hain
Haan, ye jo gehri kaali ratein hai
Ab harr waqt khauf main rehti hai

Doo tukdo mein batti huyi
Ek kahaani ka hissa ho jese
Ek hissa jahan tum ho aur mein hu,
Ek jahan mein kahin ghum hu..
Haan, ye gehr i kaali raatein
Mere hi khyaalon se khud ko bunnta hai

Iss andhere mein…meine
Pal pal gabhra kar guzaaraa hai
Haan tere chodke jaane ka khayal mujh mein paala hai
Iss andhere se jyada tera naahona,
Na jaane kyun itna khalta hai
Ye gehri kaali raaton mein
Mujhe harr baar tera wajood milta hai

Saaya koi, aahat koi
Harr lamha jese mujhe gheree hai
Tere yaadon ka harr ek kissa
Iss gehri kaali raat mein mujhe chedhe hai

Iss andhere se jyada, haan mujhe mere andar ka darr sataata
hai
Kaho toh, zara bataao…
Inn gehri kaali raaton mein..
Tu kyun itna yaad aata hai

Ye gehri kaali raatein hai

Jo sapno se shuru hua karti thi
Ab bas aaram maangti hai,
Iss andhere mein ghoom hona
Iss andhere mein sukoon khojna chaahti hai

Yeh jo gehri kaali raatein hai
Tere naa hone ki duaa maangti hai…
Yeh jo gehri kaali raatein hai..
Mujhe mere sapno se durr karti hai.
Haan, ye jo gehri kaali raatein hai
Ab harr waqt khauf main rehti hai

The Darkness, Oh Lord! Paid A Price..

When the worlds collided and smashed each other
Someone out there
Blamed the darkness forever

The darkness, oh lord!
Paid a price …
Unknowingly, became a villain..
For everything that wasn't nice…
However, tell me,
Dear reader,
What do you think?

Did the darkness lead you to depression indeed?

I see you grieve, in these hollow nights.
Looking for answers..
Alone, with your silent cries!

Yes, the dark nights… kept qui et for you
For years didn't murmur any word.
Yet this darkness, oh lord!
Paid a price..
It became a villain,
For everything that wasn't right.

The darkness knew nothing about love or ease
Still comforted you, gave you sleep and dreams..
Oh lord, why did it pay the price?
For it was so lonely, all the time..
Yet it became a villain,
For everything that wasn't light.

As everyday…every night,

When the worlds collided and smashed each other
Someone out there
Blamed the darkness forever.

Bandhuli Chatterjee

A true believer in 'Poems, prayers and promises'...Often drunk in love, literature and nature.
P.S-Official pursuer of literature (M.A in English;B.ed), currently teaching in a respected institution.

Bedtime Story

Come come now y'a all---
Let's sit around the fire,
And cuddle up some warmth,
Before the pyres rise higher!

I'll tell y'a all a story--
And keep you lured,
Till sleep creeps in---
And numbs your cure.

Once, there were seven big wolves--
Looking out for fights,
Snarling at each other--
Biting with every might!

One such member,
Of the eastern wolves,
Once---
Juggled with a dark prowess,
With ends unknown.

But drunk in malice--
He shrieked and laughed,
Unleashing the power--
That pale,old maniac!

And now my dearies---
The leftover of my fairies,
So in love with the lies--
Do y'a know,how it feels?
To be dipped in
The bleak cold ice?

The evil mistress---
Though positive's her name
Will ravage all---- real soon---
Being robbed of shame!

Come, come now y'a all---
Let's sit around the fire,
And dream of unicorns,
With vultures creeping nearer.

The "Dark Lady"

Amidst the piles of broken jars--
Sat she, lonely and afar,
Parted lips, smiling and profane
Poured,the 'Dark Lady',
An yearning strain--
Musing the bard,who's long gone--
The one who sang for her dusk,
In his dawn.

Now the waning moon,
Mocks her skin.
Whispering to her the passing hours,
In a dark, dingy inn.

Behold her--- the 'Other'!
Tossed on the edge and left to smother--
Oh! How she learns---
To fake a smile and to stiffle a shudder!

Thus fumbling amidst her strain,
 She smiles---
Moving around, collecting jars,
Of lustful eyes.

In the perspective of the recent Covid19 pandemic, let us try and take a glance at the dark dimension of the ongoing human slaughter.

Upside-Down

Have you seen the reverse side?
Chaotic-cosmos there hides---
Of what was lost,
And what was uprooten,
Lies there---
Numbered and written!
In Scarlet dots,
Etched on the earthly skin---
That stifled a cry---
When the raging fire,
Burnt her sheen!

Do you dare?
To look back and count?
All the dark sins---
Mounting in amount!
Oh! For how long,
Could you've fooled around,
With the 'May Day'--
To be turned---
To a battle ground!

And now it's started--
The playful slaughter,
The "Knock-Knock" game,
Death's own---designed disaster!
Soon--- laughing in joy--
He'll brush his cloak,
(In all good humour,)
Against the rosy cheeks
Of yet an, another...!

Don't be stressed now,

Oh, my dear,
This's nothing but,
Earth's own
Reverse disaster!
She'll cleanse herself,
And smile,
passing by---
'Darling Death', her only ally!

Thus-----
Let's meet again, in the upside-down---
When we're done with----
All the fury,
And all the frown.
And the only thing,
That'd fly in the air---
Is---
"Fair is foul,
And,
Foul is fair"!

Divyanshu Rai

Divyanshu Rai , A guy pursuing B. tech in cs branch , native of prayagraj , much fond of penning verses , what I strive for to create a   maze to influence , appreciate and spread optimism that give birth to my longing @penmyidea now my belonging forever !Just like sunrises and sunset and moon comes at night be hopeful be determined ,be like season, flow with the time to show your best and get your best.

Darkness The Shadow!!

A prevailing silence spread all over
The tik-tok, tik-tok of a clock can be listened
Darkness, Darkness everywhere
Not able to reflect, Not able to see
Just sitting silently and waiting
For the moment of light over darkness
Old memories just pass by
Something someone whispered
But who we don't know
When I asked to myself
Mind replied when you were all covered with Darkness
Darkness, Darkness everywhere
The darkness they said darkly everywhere
Not able to see anyone
Darkness when I found when you were
Fighting with your mind
A black hole of our internal mind which encompass
everything
When humanity is on the verge of an end.
Darkness I found
Which just covers the whole
 Nation like a dark blanket
Dark and Dark everywhere
Which stops your thinking
Stops your emotion
So that there cannot be more rotation
Rotation of yourself
Rotation of thoughts
Rotation of life
Rotation of journey ...
And by like that, we spend hours of darkness
Sitting bending our head
Losing ourselves in somewhere

Like particles moving in the galaxy
Somewhere for something,
Dark and Dark everywhere
But for every failure there is success
For every cause, there is a reason
Like that for dark there is light
Which when enters the galaxy make everything bright
Ends the darkness
And make everyone reflect themselves in the sparkling of
light
To wake up from someone
 for something
To enlighten the life of ours
A decision cannot be ours
But choice can be
So choose want to be a light
Or just want to get lost somewhere in Darkness
Choose wisely
Choose precisely
Be the sparkling of light
For your darkness
Be the sun!
Be the ray!

Iti Verma

Iti Verma is a research scholar, currently pursuing PhD in Management from Dayalbagh   Educational Institute, Agra. She realized her writing skills when she was in class 12th. Since then, she has been quietly jotting down her heart feelings in the form of poems, quotes, articles and short stories. Besides writing, Iti derives happiness in do ing paintings, trying new food recipes, reading novels, and teaching. Her ultimate goal is to bring a positive change in this world through her words and actions. Feel free to connect with her on her insta id: prakrati.iti

My Fears

Thoughts are changing day by day.
Don't know even what to say.

Getting confused and afraid too.
Don't know how to back out too.

Making myself through the dangerous way
Don't know even what to say.

Situations are such that lead me to this way
I don't know how to keep away.

Risk is all along the way.
I know nothing, except to pray.

God, give me way! God, give me way!
My fears are increasing day by day.

Am I wrong? Am I right?
This question strikes me everyday.

No Hope, No ray.
Don't know the right way.

Speechless and nervous,
all along the way.

Fear in my heart,
Nothing left to say.

Don't know where,
I got struck in the way.
Fears too much, have struck in my mind,
Diverted I am, Don't know how to rewind.

My fears, My fears, they bring me tears.
Don't know why I am walking this way.

Nobody to guide, Nobody to share.
Am I walking on some wrong way?

The way seems long, the risk too high.
I fear I will die, if I fly too high.
Giving Yourself Confidence

My voice should not shiver.
My thoughts should never waver.

My confidence should be unmoving.
My faith in myself remains forever.

My principles are my guidelines.
My rules will not be given up.

Situations can make me stronger.
But let not them make me weaker.

My circumstances should not affect me.
Neither can they depress me.

I will not give up on my dreams.
I will remain firm in my stream.

My self respect remains my priority.
My happiness is my necessity.

Hunting for peace, aiming for good.
I have to move on as much as I could.

Manya Arora

Manya Arora thanks her parents and friends to always letting her pursue her dreams. She is a writer who mostly engrosses herself in other's place and writes down her feelings. She is likely to write about love and other phases of a life.

The Mistake Was All Mine.

I'm sorry I came to your life
I'm sorry I wanted your time
I hope now you are fine
I'm sorry for thinking you to be mine
I'm sorry for loving you
I'm sorry for not deserving you
I'm sorry for praying for you
I'm sorry for all was my fault
I thought myself to be the salt
To add the best flavour to your life
But I forgot excess of anything spoils everything
Maybe excess of me ruined everything
THE MISTAKE WAS ALL MINE
I'm sorry for every line
I ever spoke to make you feel mine
I'm sorry for my words
I Know I am a nerd
I'm totally absurd
I do spoke without thinking
& That's the reason my love ship is sinking
I'm sorry but I never meant to hurt you
To make you feel bad
I'm sorry for being the reason of your sadness
I'm sorry for loving you with such madness
For coming to your life
Maybe my coming was meaningless
But I promise you
Now that I am leaving
I won't be giving you any pain
I'll leave just as a drop of rain
You won't be finding my existence or my name
I'm sorry for being a WIERD GAME

The One-Sided Love

Sabke samne khul kar haste hai
Akele hote hi khul kar rote hai
Har waqt yaad kar usse
Mann mei ye sochte hai
Akhir kya kami hai hum mei jo usse hum na paa sakte hai
Par ek hi qwahish se jeete hai
Chahe kuch bhi ho jaye
Humari jaan hi kyu na chali jaye
Upar se bhi usee muskuratien hi dekhe
Kyuki wo humare dil mei baste hai
Maana usee kadr nahi
Alag humare raste hai
Phir bhi uski galiyon se guzar
Uski ek hi jhalak k liye taraste hai
Khuda sb ke hai
Ek na ek din meri mohabbat ko bhi sahara denge
Fark bas itna hoga ki jab tak wo hume smjhenge
Tab tak mei unke liye hui mohabbat hum dil mei kahi dafn kar denge
Har baar dil awara ho
Unke dil ko dhoondhta hai
Unke sath Zindagi guzarne ke spne
Ye dil har pal boonta hai
Jo ek pal bhi unke sath guzarta hai
Ye dil unke dil se judne lgta hai
Par chuki unhe wo nai dikhta hai
Ye dil jud kar bhi toot jata hai
Ishq karne se phle suna tha
Ishq buri ek latt hai boht dard milega
Par ishq tha sachha isiliye mann ne kaha
Ab ishq unse ladane ka ye faisla nai badlega
Abhi bhi dil dukhta hai
Par uski hasi se alag hi kism ka sukoon milta hai

Uske liye khilona hi sahi par kuch toh hu
Ye sochkar dil rote hue bhi hasta hai!

Nishant Sobti

Nishant Sobti is a part time writer who completed his graduation in Bachelor's of Commerce (BCOM) from Mumbai University.
He lives in Thane, Mumbai.
He writes the feelings, the emotions of millions of people that they might be going through in their everyday life.

Mai Ek Naqaab Hoon

Ek aisa naqaab, jo apne dard ko chupa raha hai isme khud ko samaa raha hai...

Apne aansoo ko akele mein baarish ki boondon ki tarah gira raha hai, aur bhari mehfil mein muskura raha hai.

Sabke saamne kehta hai ki woh   bilkul theek hai, par yeh toh wohi jaanta hai ki woh andar se kitna toota hua hai.

Yeh dard mere nass nass mein jo bhara hua hai ,yeh meri jeene ki saari khwaishon ko andar hi andar dabaa raha hai.

Aisa lagta hai jaise ek aag lagi hai mujhme, mere poore   body mein....
Jise na mai bhujha paa raha hoon, aur na mai uss aag ko seh paa raha hoon.

Bahar se jo shanti, jo muskurahatein mere chehre par dikh rahi hai....
Woh muskurahat mere dil mein, meri zindagi mein akelepan se hue andhere ki nishaani hai.

Shayad ek aisi deewar maine khud ke liye bana li hai ki ab jaise mujhe kisi ki zaroorat nahi..... Mai akela hi theek hoon.

Shayad ab mujhe ye akelapan hi accha lagta hai....bhale hi mujhe akelapan andar se poora khalta hai, mujhe khatam kar raha hai.
Par ab kisi ke meri zindagi mein aane ki koi umeed bachi nahi hai.

Jab tak meri baaki ki zindagi rahegi.....yeh darr bhi mere sath hi rahega...

Bass ek aas hai, ek sapna zaroor hai ki kisi din koi mere pass aakar mera yeh naqaab hataakar, mujhe benaqaab kar de...

Abhi Zindagi Baaki Hai

Kya hua ?
Kuch theek nahi lagg raha na...
Mann mein ek bechaini si hai,
Dimaag khaali khaali sa lag raha hai.
Kisi se baat karne ka mann bohot kar raha hai par kisse karein? Kya baat karein? Agar maine   message kiya to kya saamne se reply aayega?Yeh sawaal bhi mann mein hamesha sath hai...
Ek akelapan sa lag raha hai ki koi sath nahi.
Logon Ko bass yeh hi dikhate jaa rahe hai ek fake smile ka emoji social media chats pe daalke, jaise sab theek hai, Khair chhodo koi baat nahi...
Bass wait karte hai ki koi humein message kare, call kare yeh sochkar ki chalo kisi se baat karke hum apna dil behla lenge, mann ko mana lenge, thoda muskura lenge ki chalo ek din ke liye sahi baat toh hui kisise...
 Par woh baat kabhi hoti hi nahi.
Din poora hone tak phir khudko akela paata hoon,
par harr baar kahin shant jagah par jaakar sukoon se sochta hoon...
Aisa kyun hota hai?
Par uss kyu ka jawaab kayin Baar Nahi milta.
Lekin phir bhi khudko samjhata hoon ki koi baat nahi, yehi to zindagi hai... Mujhe haarna nahi hai, mai strong hoon...
Abhi toh poori zindagi baaki hai yaar
 Abhi mai thokar khaake gira hoon, lekin ruko zara, sabar karo, abhi mera uthna baaki hai.
Thoda khudko jhuka liya hai, par abhi mera seena taanke chalna baaki hai....
Bohot ro liya abhi hasna aur hasaana baaki hai.
Abhi meri zindagi baaki hai...
Abhi mera jeena baaki hai.

Priyanka K. Tiwari

Priyanka had a poetic disposition from childhood on. Her first poem appeared in a newspaper, when she was 8. She has written many poems in English and Hindi. To her, poetry is " Words that breathe, Emotions that bleed". A graduate in Biotechnology, she is currently associated with the field of HR - Organizational Psychology. Travelling, photography and reading are her passions. Insta ID   - @pri_at_insta

Aftermath

The catastrophe has passed
As every nightmare does,
But woe! The scars so deep
And the memories so painful
Will give pangs in life
Now and forever.....
The ground beneath the feet
Has given way; the sky
Shall be the only roof
Those laughing faces have faded
And destiny has evaded
Left me alone on a lonely path
A path so dark,
A path so dreary,
And dawn is miles away......
I know not where the road may lead
To sunlight;
Or...
To yet another twilight?
The questions are many,
And the answers....none!
Tears sting my eyes
Tears of agony, tears of pain,
And they tell not lies.
Hope is in vain...
But oh! For the familiar touch of warmth!
To soothe my wounds...
But here's a chilly wind
To stab my lonesome heart
Amplifying my utter utter
Solitude,
My loneliness,
Broadcasting my helplessness,

My forlornness,
My misfortune.....
The deafening silence, the maddening stillness,
Pierce through my ears,
Echoing the silent sobs of my heart,
My mute laments, my hushed sighs....
The deep dark stretch above
In darker hues still
Reflects and mirrors
My meaningless,
My dreaded
Tomorrow.
The vast openness, the interminable space
Suffocates and stifles my soul...
And my existence as a whole.
Where are those smiles?
Where are those sighs?
That filled my life
That looked aeons ago...
Is this a life?
Call it life....
It is a memoir
Of those happy memories
That will now ever look like a dream...
And pain-laden flashbacks
It's a tomb
Of buried hopes
And aspirations...
It's a kaleidoscope
Of conflicting emotions
And utter frustrations...
It's a song
Of eternal separation,
Of perpetual pain
And

Melancholy ineffable...
I find myself
Lonely
Lonely in this crowded world
But I see the twinkling stars above
And in them, those faces
That had once sustained me...
And now their radiance
Will guide me through the murky night
To yet another day?

Renukuntla Murali

Renukuntla Murali is a bilingual poet in Telugu & English. He did M.A.English. M.Phil.B.Ed.,M.Sc.Psychology, Dip in light music. He is a prolific writer in English.He was born at Vangapahad a   village in warangal dist., but settled in Jangoan city&dist.,Telangana state.He is working as Lflhm at Mpps Gurijakunta MDL Cherial,Siddipet dist.,TS state. He has written 550 poems in English & 250 in Telugu. He is the centurion poet both in Telugu & Engl   ish. He has got 35 National & international awards& 325 appreciation certificates for his writings in English. He is the best writer awardee&champion of English honoured by PB Publishers&Nazm -e-hayath a well known literary organisations.He has written 10 b ooks on spoken English & grammar, some are available in Amazon. He is the international English Poet,Writer&Author. He is the Director for Sanath Institute of English&spoken English, life skills trainer. His poems were published in 55 anthologies.

Death is certain

" Death is certain in
This world
All living beings
Born and certain to
Death on one day
No body is exempted
From the clutches of
The death,

Life is a drama, we are
All the actors, until
The portion of our part
We have to wait and Act,

Life is like a bubble
Life is like waves of
The ocean
Life is like thorns of
The rose,

Life span is short
We are now here
After death we have
To leave from here
And go to hell or
Heaven that is
That is depends
Upon our activities
In this world
We go to another
World waiting room
For us,

In the words of Aristotle
'Man is a social animal'
We must live and
Cooperate and
Coordinate with each
Other with affection,

Don't be envy and
Jealousy with others
Be happy and help
Others who are need
Of a anything,

Nothing will come
With us after death
Everything is left
Here, we have to
Leave everything
Including family,
Friends, assets
Gold, land, beauty
Except our
Knowledge."

Ritwika Ghosh

Ritwika Ghosh, born on August 2, 1997, belongs to a Bengali family. She lives in Kolkata, West Bengal. She loves to write poetries. She is an English Hons. graduated student from Calcutta University. Writing poems on various theme is her passion.

Darkness Of My Life !!!

Sometimes its' so nice to be alone
No one to interrupt our thoughts
No one to make demand of our time.
Sometimes the world seems to rush
And the silence of no one there
Soothes the ill of the day.
There are times when we have nothing to say
And really don't care to hear another's voice
Times when, if we wanted to sing out, dance about
Just act like a fool.
There's no one to tell you so.
Those times are so precious.

There's nothing I want more
Than to hear your voice, feel your touch.
But sadly it is one of those times
And I.....
I am alone
And you are not.
It's the darkness of my life.

Sanjay Naik

He is Sanjay Naik from Kharagpur State of West bengal, completed his graduation from Economics (Hons). Writer from heart, Passionate about singing. Through the platform of Anthology he wants to spread love & positivity among the readers. Wants to heal readers heart by his magical words. He writes poems , Quotes etc in his leisure time. Instagram: - @the_poetry_wo

अंधकार – रोशनी की पूरक

अंधकार को अज्ञान का प्रतीक समझना स्वाभाविक है
ये हमारी सकारात्मक सोच पर हावी हो जाती है
जिंदगी के पथ पर भटका देती है
पर उजाले के अर्थ को भला अंधकार बिना
कैसे समझा जा सकता है
ये एक दूसरे के बिल्कुल पूरक हैं।

तृप्ति के एहसास को समझने के लिए
भूखे रहना जरूरी है उसी तरह
रोशनी के महत्व को समझने के लिए
अंधकार को जानना भी उतना ही आवश्यक है
ये दोनों ही जीवन के अभिन्न हिस्से हैं
एक का मूल्य दूसरे के बिना समझ पाना मुमकिन नहीं।

यह सत्य है कि सूर्य के बिना पहले सृष्टि में अंधकार था
अंधकार और प्रकाश मिलकर ही चक्र पूरा करते हैं
हमारा जीवन दिन रात की तरह ही होती है
यही सृष्टि का नियम है जिस पर हमें चलना है
आंखें बंद करके ही साधना की जा सकती है
ये अंधकार ही है जो ध्यान को केंद्रित और एकाग्रता लाती है।

Darkness – Complement Of Light

It is natural to consider darkness as a symbol of ignorance
It dominates our positive thinking
Wanders off the path of life
But without the darkness of the meaning of light
How can be understood
These complement each other perfectly.

To understand the feeling of fulfilment
The same way it is to be hungry
To understand the importance of light
It is equally important to know the darkness
Both of these are integral parts of life
It is not possible to understand the value of one without the other.

It is true that there was darkness in the first creation without the sun
Darkness and light together complete the cycle
Our life is like day and night
This is the law of the universe that we have to follow
Meditation can be done by closing eyes
It is darkness that brings focus and concentration.

Siddharth Agarwal

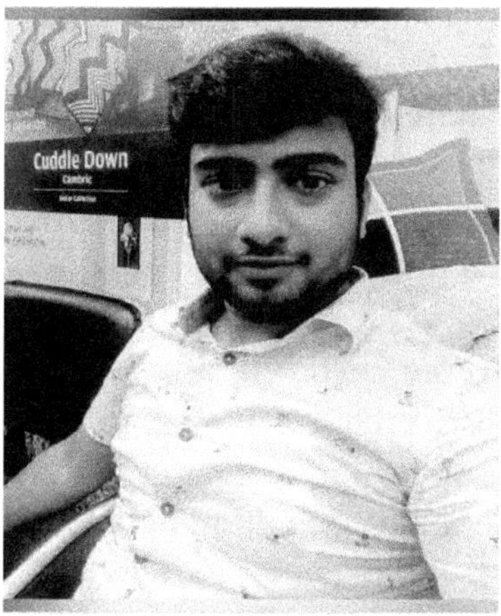

Siddharth is a simple guy who likes to play with words...
He can make you feel exactly what he writes...

Tum Hi Batao..

Us raat ko kaise bhula paaye ham tum hi batao..
Janmdin tumhara tha aur tohfa bhi tumne hi mujhe diya,
Us karz ko kaise chukaye ham, tum hi batao….

Tohfa bh idiya to aisa diya ki zindagi bhar hame yaad rahegi,
In yaadon ko kaise mitaye ham tum hi batao…..

Chhap gayi hai dil me wo tasvir jab tumhare haathon me kisi
aur ke haath ko dekha tha,
Tumhari nazron ko kisi aur ke nazron se milte dekha tha,
Us tasvir ko kaise mitaye ham tum hi batao…..

Jis jagah ham apne khubsurat lamhe saath bitate the
Us jagah par aaj kisi aur ko dekhkar khud ko kaise rok paaye
ham tum hi batao…

Aaj hafto baad tumhe hamari yaad aayi hai,
Kuch kasar shayad abhi baaki reh gayi thi jo waqt tumhe
mere paas layi hai,
Aur ham tumhare kuch calls kya nahi uthaye tumhe rona tak
aa gaya..
Uss raat ko ham kitna roye honge ye bhi ab tum hi
batao…………

Suriyanshi Mishra

My name is Suriyanshi Mishra. I'm student and a NCC cadet and I'm All India Ranked Rifle Shooter. I'm writing since am 10 years old. Writing is my passion. Ink stained paper makes me feel so much happy. I think paper has more patience than people so whenever I feel depressed or lonely I start writing. Since I never planned that anyone is going to read my writings but now I'm so encouraged to show my writings to the other. Filling white pages with the ink is the best therapy of me and I feel so blessed to have such a talent to put down my feelings into words.

I'm In Love –

Finally you leave me after 5 years of relationship
and after you who says that I'm not in love?
Yes I'm in love
Yes I'm in love
But this time not with any guy's soul.
I'm in love with every single moment when I admire the sky,
When I'm looking at the colorful sky, I'm In love with that
bright moon who is encouraging me at every moment to
shine brighter.
I'm in love with the darkness of night.
I'm in love the way I smile for myself.
I'm in love the way I'm holding myself.
I'm in love the way I care for myself.
Yes I'm in love but this time the person is me
Yes I'm in love again and I'm so happy.

खुद की तलाश-

मैं अक्सर खुद को खो देती हू,
और फिर खुद को ढूंढने निकल पड़ती हूँ,
कुछ सवाल है जो मुझे सोने नही देते उन्केजवाबो की तलाश में
एक सफर पर चल पड़ती हूँ ।
और हर बारी यही सोचती हू के इस बार किसी के बारे में नही
सोचूंगी।
बहुत हो गया अब
आज़ादी चाहिए मुझे,
सबसे, सबकेखयलो से
बहुत हो गया अब
मुझे अब अपने लिये जीना है,
कुछ करना है कुछ पाना है
और सबकोभुल जाना हैं
और ना जाने कब यही सब सोचते हुये मेरा दिन निकल जाता है
और अखिरमेफिरसेसबकी प्यारी बातों का गुल्दस्ता मेरे दिल में रह
ही जाता हैं।
निकली थी में खुद को ढूंढने लेकिंनसबमें फिर से उलझ कर रह गई
नाह खुद को ढूंढ पाई और ना सबकीबात्तेंभुल पाई इसलिये अभी
भी मैं अपनी तलाश मे हूँ, अपनी तलाश में हूँ ।

मेरी मुस्कुराहट

आज फिर दिन भर सबसे सुनती रही की मैं हर वक़्त
मुस्कुरातीरहती हूँ।
घर आकर आइना देखा तो में हँस पडीक्युकी आज भी मै
सबकोबुधू बना कर घर लौट आई।
कुछ देर बाद मेरी हसी गायब हो गई और मेरी नजरें झुक गई।
आंखेआँसूओ से भर गई अब खुद को में केसेयकीदिलाऊ की मै
खुश हूँ।
मैं आज भी खुद से झूठ बोलना सिख नहीं पाई हूँ।
आइने की तरफ पीठ करके खड़ी हो गई, आज भी में खुद को सच
का आइना दिखा नहीं पाई

T. Priyadharshini

She's Priyadharshini. An english literature student. She loves to read and write. She's engrossed in writing poems, blogs and quotes. A budding writer and a movie lover too.

The Darkest Minutes Of My Life

It was 10.45 pm,
I opened my somnolent eyes;
By hearing the buzzing sound of the phone,
It was my friend.

I picked it up and answered in my drowsy voice,
The voice over the other end was dreary and said,
"The results are out, you can check it out."
For a moment, I sensed my heart beat stopped and resumed
beating.

My fingers trembled,
My whole body shuddered out of fear,
Anxiety was written all over my face,
Though I accumulated all my courage.

I checked it out! I couldn't make it! I failed!
I sensed a huge pressure inside my heart,
My mind was completely blank,
Hot tears ran down and soaked my cheeks.

I felt all alone,
Silence encircled me,
I was inert and stock-still,
All of a sudden I felt my world was completely darkened.

All my day and night endeavours gone useless,
I looked upon the night skies;
It was sombre and starless,
I stood like a dead duck.

The miscarriage I faced is merely nothing;

Infront of other debacles,
But it created a horrowing impact within me,
This was the most darkest minutes of my life.

My own expectation darkened my inner-self,
It hauled me down,
It drenched my soul with darkness,
I lost myself in the darkness called 'Expectation'.

'Expectation' is the most darkest aspect of human,
It can daub one's life with darkness,
It can splinter one's credence and;
It can shatter one's intention.

For others this is just an exam result; but for me it's life!
Not only for me but for many,
Exam result is still a frightful figure among all,
It shoves them to a distressing point.

It pushes them into the most horrific darkness called
'Suicide'.
It has taken away innumerable innocent souls,
Still the death toll is increasing,
This is the real darkness.

But baby! Stars can shine only in the darkness,
Though you are pressed to a point of annihilation,
Just ignite your soul with 'Optimism',
Then even in the pitch of darkness;
You can barely see a streak of lustre called 'Hope'.

Taniya Khemchandani

Taniya Khemchandani is an ordinary girl from the city Kota.Her hobbies are singing and writing.She loves to observe things in her life.She is passionate about writing and expressing her feelings into words.

You can contact her through

Instagram: @taniyakhemchandani

Facebook:

Taniya khemchandani

Snapchat:

Iamtaniyaaaaa

Twitter:

@IamTaniyaaaaa

Gmail:

taniyakhemchandani@gmail.com

Understanding Depression

I am tired
Tired of the constancy
The constancy of judgement
Tired of hiding who I am
Tired of trying to stay strong

I am tired
Tired of pretending
Pretending to be happy
When all I want to do is cry
Tired of not being able to let go,
Let go of all the emotions and pain that consume me
Tired of feeling worthless

I am tired
Tired of remembering
Remembering how I used to be so happy
Tired of the blame
The blame I put on myself daily
Tired of the anger

I am tired
Tired of crying
Crying in the shower,so nobody can hear.
Tired of the fear,
The fear of being judged all the time.
Tired of failing

I am tired
Tired of holding on when all I want to do is give up
Tired of being tired
Tired of being me

Pain Of Depression

You would never know it
The pain which I feel
Because in the light of day
It almost is not real

Sure,I will play,I will laugh
I will sing some songs
But that pain is always lurking
Because its been here all along

And when the darkness come
With all its consuming power
It slowly takes my soul
Hour by dreadful hour

But you know, it tells me
That I am strong enough
They swear that it will get
Better one day….
They tell me "You will be happy one day"
All you need to do is fight

And so I act along
I play my part…
While this darkness
Slowly breaks my heart.

It's hidden in those bullies,
Who torture,use their
Words like weapons to
Destroy self esteem

It can cause someone to

Just give up,
To lose all strength
To fight.

It can annihilate one's soul
And make them take their life

Depression is a vulture
That will make anyone its prey,
There is no one who deserves it,
And there is no one to blame it.

We don't need to make a judgement,
All we need is to be aware
Those who suffer through this pain,
Just need the world to care.

Trupti Rajesh.Hangirgekar

TRUPTI RAJESH.HANGIRGEKAR.
From Belgaum, Karnataka.
Born on 2nd September 2003.Currenty studying 4th Semester Diploma Computer Science & Engineering.She has interest in Sports & Love nature. Not a well Professional writer but it became her Love all because of Inspiration of her PARENTS,Two SISTER'S ...And two more important people,her God gifted Friends Aarbaz Khan & Preksha Pawale.Who always supported her to aspire higher goals..She is also a Co-author of Books:
 "Unsaid Goodbyes" By 'Vaishnavi Jadhav',who is also a wave of inspiration to her..
"zikar-e-jajbaat" By Khushi Navneet &
"Keetle of Poetry" By Prasad R.B...

"WRITING IS WAY OF EXPRESSING LOVE WHICH CAN'T BE SPOKEN"

The Cave Of Sweven Which Seemed Her Like
Nightmare

With the early darkness of thick clouds cover;
She seemed afraid of being alone.
Where her shadow hide in darkness
& life looked to be messery& hopeless.
That place was cave of nightmare
She thought,
With all hatred,pain&fear.
She saw nothing but death & darkness in every soul she ran
across,
Darkness lingered at the edges of her mind;
But with spirit in her Heart,
She saw the contrast of
Light & shadow
Creating beauty & mystery.
Seeing the infinite rainbow of fascinating colour& hues;
Lie's between the polarities of
Dark & light.
Then she believed;
This cave of nightmare,
Was just a season of awaken,
Of beauty that same charming setting sun has of that same
rising sun do.
Through darkness comes light,
Through night comes day.
Through fear comes love,
Through pain comes success.
This is a success of Human spirit;
It is not in few,
It's in everyone of you.
The Twilight of life,
Is to see the sweven in the nightmare.
And engage in adventures,
With both Darkness& light,

To experience the life in this universe.

The power of darkness

Darkness isn't always baleful;
But sometimes safe too.
There's darkness even in the womb of a women;
But there isn't any fear,
 It's instead filled with love & warmth.
And now that I have stepped out;
Found the brightness everywhere,
And ignored it's importance.
But the ignorance pushed me in the darkness,
The darkness with no hope's I thought;
Where found my shadow
Had ran away,
And it wasn't walking with me today.
With the fear of being alone,
Have learnt the strength I carry.
Which reminded me the flawless beauty of the Moon;
That shines alone with some sparking stars around,
In the devilish dark sky.
The moon awakened the confidence within,
Which was lost in the beginning.
This adventure of Darkness & Light,
Thought me the lesson for life.
"Either be in dark or in light
The brightness that sparks from within;
Is only torch that leads
You all the way of life."

बचपन में जिस अंधेरे मे डर लगता था,
आज उसी अंधेरे मेसुखुन मिलता हैं!"

Venessa Albuquerque

Venessa Albuquerque is a Graduate in Science in Anaesthesia Technology from South Goa. She spends more words on Poetry, but does   like writing Fiction, short stories and Blogs. She prefers the Ink and Paper more than the screen as she says 'It just comes naturally'. She wants to be recognized by her writings. Her Parents have supported her constantly and that's why we say Family is '   Constant'. She has also been featured in 'Shades of Love' Anthology and other Anthologies. She is a constant blogger on Sweek.

Through The Darkness

Through the darkness
A shimmering light I see
Way down the timeline
I don't know, where
Would I be ?

Through the darkness
I kept going my way
No other way I'd see
I thought this is what
Would be my destiny

Through the darkness
Comes a sense of independence
The will to lead yourself somewhere
The light you see far away
Is somewhere within you

Through the darkness
One thing I knew
I must keep going through
Destiny will be waiting
This isn't the end

Through the darkness
I finally succeed
Cause Success isn't destiny
Success is a Journey
Darkness is just a phase
Everything beyond is Bright !

kAID HAI KAHIN MUJH MEIN

Ek khayal sa aaya mann mein
Chadh gayya who dil mein
Kaise nikalun use mere andar se
Kaid hai who kahin us duniya mein
Kaidhaikahin who mujhmein

Kaid hai kissi ke yaadon mein hum
Kaid kar liya kissi ko yaadon mein humne
Es kaid ko hi apni duniya samajh li humne
Kaid mein bhi parchayee ka saath dhoondh
Kaid hai kahin hum khud mein

Who nazar jo mili thi pehle
Reh gayyi tasveer mann mein
Kaise na sochun uske bare mein
Kaid hai who kahin zehen mein
Kaid hai kahin who mujh mein

Kaid hai kissi ke baton mein hum
Kaid kar liya kissi ko baton mein humne
Es kaid se niklein toh kuch aur sunayi de
Kaid mein bhi ek dhun sun li jo humne
Kaid hai kahin hum khud mein

Ek Ek dard tumhara diya gayya
Lekin ek katra bhi tumhara nahi
Seh liya hum dono ne utna hi
Kaid hai who dard mere dil mein
Kaid hai kahin who mujh mein

No Words To Say

Even now when I think of you
I have lots of memories to tell
But all I know about myself is
I have no words to say

Hardly I remember you now
I tell myself not to cry
But all what I say is
I have no words to say

Whenever I hear your name
I feel like telling everything about you
But all what comes to my mind is
I have no words to say

If I ever see you
It feels like telling you everything
Feel like hearing something from you
But all what you say is…
I have no words to say

Yashika Karamchandani

Yashika Karamchandani is a literature enthusiast currently completing her studies and lives in Neemuch, M.P. She   is a dreamer by heart and strongly believes in Dreams do come true. An incipient writer and a budding author of a recently published novel, "Dreams do come true" and also a co author in more than 6 anthologies. She loves to play guitar, read books, explore new places and meet new people. She believes in living her life to the fullest.

Unimaginatively Imaginative

And sometimes you feel nothing,
Just nothing, a lost way, or a fake hope, an undying faith, or
haunting nightmares.
Just stuck between nowhere and somewhere
Trying to find yourself in this crowd,
Life keeps on going,
Memories keeps on fading,
People turning into strangers and strangers into best friends
for life,
And sometimes you feel nothing
Just nothing, an unknown fear, or an unending grief,
pretending smile, or hiding tears.
And then you are back to normal in a while.
But sometimes you feel nothing, just empty, vacant in your
heart like something is broken inside you which can never be
fixed.
For a moment you are fighting back emotions, knowing
nothing about yourself forget about the world,
For a moment you are praying for impossibles, for miracles.
For a moment you realize your dreams come shattering down
in front of your eyes, for a moment you wake up, and see a
new reality… naah which is far away from your dreams,
For a moment your life is fast forwarded,
For a moment you are paused, you are stuck, you are dead,
you are lost,
And then you are back to normal
In a while…

Sometimes In Life.

Sometimes some things happens and you are just paused for a while, not sad, not angry, like emotionless you are stuck at that one moment. Forbidden to remember, terrified to forget, it's a h ard line to walk. Your mind over thinking like hell, yours eyes numb and you are choked.
Nothing is actually wrong at that moment, but nothing feels to be right even. But that's how you are! And sometimes you need to accept the fact that not all things can go the way you want them to.

You

There come a time in everyone's life when everything around you appears to be dark, darkness everywhere, you try to find a ray of light, a ray of hope to guide your way, you shout for any kind of familia r voice but there is deadly silence. And you don't know where to go and what to do.
Calm down at that moment, look inside. You yourself are the light you keep on searching in the world. You are that ray of hope, those words of inspiration, that hand which   will pick you up and guide your way.
Realize you are magical, you are what all you need. You are your own guardian angel. Just keep on going and leave a bit of your sparkle wherever you go in this dark world.

Zainab Shakir

Zainab Shakir, a young a uthor hailing from Banswara, Rajasthan, currently pursuing her secondary studies writes in her mean time, finding writing relaxing and also possesses skills in art and oration.

He Who Knows

Master of the gleam,
Hiding in the gloom
Is making us wonder
About the doom,
Is it the end, or
The life shall resume?

He is to deam,
If the flowers are to bloom,
The arrival of thunder,
He shall presume,
The created blunder
He shall renew

Flairs and Glairs, a platform by a student for the students. We are esteemed youth struggling to carve out our path for our future and we follow a basic mindset Since everyone is not born with all - round skills. Joining hands with people who are born to execute it with perfection is the best way to evol ve. Self -Evolution is the need of the hour but, evolving as a community is what we strive for. The initiative as kickstarted by, Founder - Mr. Shubham Shah with the motive to utilize the skillset and talent of writing has now a team of 10+ people who are ac tively participating into newer forms of learning and discovering talents among youngsters. We Provide platform and services like Publishing opportunities, Open mics, Workshops, Hands -on training. Operating with Brand Name of Flairs and Glairs (Publication House), we offer the chance of elevating a passionate writer to an esteemed author With Brand name Teekhe Zasbaaat. We bring to you an opportunity to get accustomed with the Public Speaking and Presenting of Thoughts along with regular challen ges to brush up your inking spirit. The newest initiative to extend our services we introduced in a new writing Platform- The Glittering Fables and Ink Over Tears.

We Choose to Fly Like A Falcon than to be

a Leg Pulling Crab.

To Know More: Infoline – 7781900870
Mail Us At-
flairsandglairs@gmail.com / info@flairsandglairs.in
Or Visit is at
www.flairsandglairs.com / www.flairsandglairs.in
Social Handles- @flairsandglairs @teekhezasbaaat